Ruby Jean Goes to the Dentist

First Edition

PAGE PUBLISHING, INC.
Conneaut Lake, PA

First originally published by Page Publishing 2021

ISBN 978-1-64701-325-7 (pbk)
ISBN 978-1-64701-326-4 (digital)

Printed in the United States of America

Ruby Jean Goes to the Dentist

VICKIE HAYNES-LEECH

Acknowledgments

I have to start by saying, writing and telling a story for the most part comes easy for me. Yet, becoming an author turned out to be one of the hardest things I have ever done and more rewarding than I ever could have imagined. None of this would have happened without my dearest daughter. So, first and foremost, I want to thank my ever-patient daughter Ajeenah Lateefah Haynes-Saafir. Thank you! Ajeenah, you stood by me during every struggle to fulfill my dream of becoming an author. Your patience and tough love helped me to succeed with this book. You never minded the late or early morning calls of frustration. You stood fast with encouragement and helped me *see* my talent. And, thank you for taking the time out of your tremendously busy schedule to read my unorganized first drafts…and not once change anything. You would always just respond with "Do *you* like it?", "How would you make it better?", or my favorite, "Mom, just leave it". Thank you for listening to my endless complaining that this wasn't going to happen for me and thank you for giving me endless praise—supporting me through it all. I truly have no idea what would have become of my writing had I not decided to ask you to read one of my stories. That day became the beginning of a dream come true. You are always there for me and now it's full steam ahead with my new career as an author!

To my sister Angela Shabazz-Potts, thank you for always being the person I could turn to when I just needed to vent. Your encouragement and advice always made me feel better and allowed me to look at any issue from a much clearer perspective. I appreciate our talks more than you could ever know. You are a woman of so many talents…thank you for insisting over and over again to give me a makeover. Your persistence profoundly showed how beautiful I can still be at 67 years young. Thank you so much, sis (*thister*).

To my sons Dale Jr. and Al-Adrian, who always keep me relevant in their lives and always refer to me as the "best mom ever", thank you.

To my publication coordinator, thank you for being there every step of the way. You are appreciated.

FLOUR
CHOCOLATE CHIPS

"Mommy, tomorrow I go to the dentist, can I still have dessert?"
"Sure, Ruby, just brush before bedtime like always."
That night Ruby brushed just a little longer.

While driving to the dentist, Ruby asked her mom, "Will I have the same nice dentist as before?"

"Yes," her mom replied. "Dr. Bonic is your very own dentist."

Ruby arrived at the dentist.

Everyone greeted her. "Hi, Ruby." "Hello, Ruby, great to see you again."

Ruby smiled her biggest smile. "Hi," she replied with a wave.

"You can have a seat. The doctor will see you shortly," said the lady at the front desk.

VROOM!
VROOM!

Ruby and her mom sat down. There was a little boy playing with his truck, and Ruby noticed that she knew him from church; he was in her Bible class. Ruby looked around. A little girl in a yellow dress was reading a book. Ruby thought the dress was very pretty. There were lots of books for kids on the table.

Ruby asked her mom, “Can I get one?”

“Sure,” her mom said.

Ruby picked a book all about puppies—big ones, little ones, brown ones, and even puppies with spots.

“Mommy, you think we could get a puppy? These puppies are so cute.”

Her mom just smiled. “They are pretty cute,” she replied.

As Ruby looked through the book, the office door opened.

Dr. Bonic called out, “Ruby Jean.”

Ruby looked at her mom. “That’s me.”

Dr. Bonic replied, “Hello, Ruby. You want to follow me?”

Ruby walked up to the dentist then waved to her mom. Dr. Bonic smiled and told her mom, “It won’t take long. This will just be a checkup.”

Ruby followed him. They passed two rooms before Dr. Bonic told Ruby, “Here we go, Ruby. Step right this way please.”

Ruby entered a room with lots of pictures on the wall, a large chair, and sink with a counter filled with things to help make your teeth healthy and strong.

Ruby laughed at the biggest bottle of mouthwash she had ever seen standing on the floor; it was as tall as she was.

"Dr. Bonic," Ruby said, "is there mouthwash in there?"

Dr. Bonic answered with a chuckle, "No, Ruby, it's only pretend."

Ruby laughed. "It sure is big!"

Dr. Bonic lowered the chair with a push of a button and asked Ruby to be seated. Ruby got up in the chair as a pretty lady walked into the room.

Dr. Bonic told the lady, “Rose, this is Ruby Jean. She is here for a checkup today.”

“How are you today Ruby Jean and what a nice name.”

“Thank you,” Ruby replied.

Rose helped get Ruby ready. She tied a small paper cloth around Ruby’s neck.

MOUTH
WASH

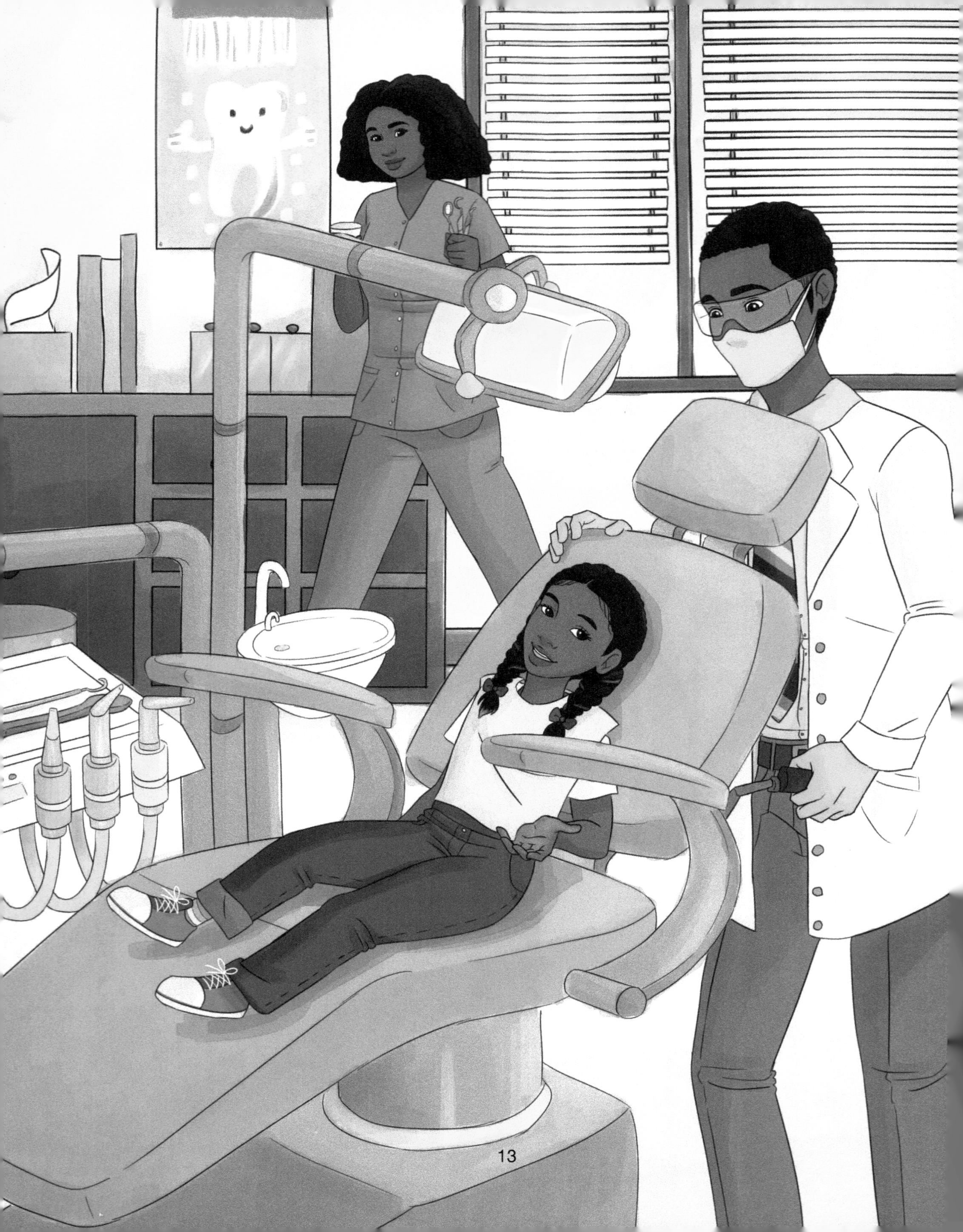

As Ruby sat there, she watched Rose walk about the room opening cabinets and drawers getting things for the checkup.

Dr. Bonic puts on his gloves and special glasses, walks over, and moves the handle on the chair—it lays Ruby back.

“Okay, are we ready?” asked Dr. Bonic. “Can you open wide for me, Ruby? That’s great. Now relax and let’s see.”

Finally, Dr. Bonic was done. He raised Ruby's head and put his hand up for a high-five. "Good job, Ruby. Your teeth are great. You are doing a terrific job. I will see you back in six months. Now Rose will finish up."

Rose handed Ruby a red pill. "Can you chew this up and rinse? Try not to swallow."

"Sure," Ruby replied.

Rose explained the red pill would show how well Ruby brushed her teeth. When Ruby was done, Rose handed her a mirror and said "now smile."

Ruby gave a big, happy smile and was shocked to see all her teeth were red.

She looked at Rose. "My teeth are all red."

Rose laughed. "Yes, they are, but they look great."

Ruby frowned.

Rose, in between laughter, explained, "The red pill shows all the things you may have left behind when you don't brush well, but it clearly shows you have done a good job."

Ruby was excited. She told Rose, "I can't wait to tell Grandma. She always asks me, 'Did you brush, Ruby!' My grandma is so funny."

MOUTH
WASH

And Rose and Ruby both smiled. Rose helped Ruby down from the chair. While walking out of the room, Rose stopped and opened a drawer.

"Hey! How would you like some candy for such a great checkup—sugarless, that is."

"Yes, please. Do you have cherry? That's my favorite."

Rose smiled. "Cherry it is." Rose took Ruby's hand and walked down the hall. Ruby gave her mom a big smile, and Rose asked Ruby's mom to step up to the front desk to get Ruby's next appointment.

Rose said, "Well, Ruby, we'll see you next time. Keep brushing."

On the way home, Ruby asked her mom, “Mommy, when you go to the dentist, do you get sugarless candy too?”

Mom smiled. “Yes, and I put it in my purse and save it for you.”

CPSIA information can be obtained
at www.ICGtesting.com
Printed in the USA
BVHW022110251021
619846BV00017BA/1075